The Pickle Patch Bathtub

This book is presented by
First Lady Christie Vilsack
on behalf of
Iowa Stories 2000

This book belongs to:

Thank You to Our Sponsors

IOWA STUDENT LOAN®

Prudential Financial

EAGLE
WINDOWS·DOORS

Principal Financial Group Foundation, Inc.

Principal
Financial
Group

IOWA SOYBEAN
ASSOCIATION
Expanding Opportunities. Delivering Results.

WELLS
FARGO

HOMETOWN PERRY, IOWA

HyVee

ACT

PEOPLE. PROGRESS. PRIDE.™
IOWA FARM BUREAU

citigroup

Heinz
Muscatine, Iowa

DIXON
DIXON TICONDEROGA COMPANY
"Since 1795"
A FILA COMPANY

Rotary International District 6000
Beef Products, Inc. • Casey's General Stores, Inc. • The Des Moines Register • First Data/Western Union
Freddie Mac • IOWA Telecom • Sallie Mae • SUDO CORPORATION, Sioux City, Iowa
Swiss Valley Farms, Co. • Tyson Foods, Inc. • Wells' Dairy, Inc.
Department of Cultural Affairs • Iowa Department of Education • Iowa Stories 2000 • State Library of Iowa

A Note to Families

For seven years, I've traveled across Iowa visiting with three and sometimes four generations of Iowans in schools and libraries, urging families to tell their stories aloud and to write them down. When I discovered *The Pickle Patch Bathtub*, written by Frances Kennedy, a retired sixth grade teacher from Dubuque, I knew I'd found the perfect book for Iowa's kindergarteners and their families in 2006.

This story embodies the Iowa values of setting a goal and working hard to reach it, perseverance in the face of obstacles, loyalty to family and personal sacrifice for the greater good. The book looks at managing money wisely and delayed gratification.

Frances has been an Iowa teacher for nearly 30 years, but she's also always wanted to be a writer. She has rejections saved over years of submitting manuscripts. "Sometimes you have to wait your whole life to fulfill your goal," she tells audiences. Every child in Iowa needs to hear that message. Maybe you can tell your child a story about a goal that took you a long time to reach or one you're still working to reach.

I hope that reading *The Pickle Patch Bathtub* together will encourage families to share their special family stories around the dinner table, in the car, or over the internet.

Iowa's senior citizens also love this book. They tell great stories about baths in a galvanized tub. I have posted some of their stories about bathtubs and pickles at my website (christievilsack.org).

With each book we've included a map of Iowa and a list of one family-friendly event or place in each county that will give you and your children a chance to get to know your state while spending time together. Take the map and the soy crayons, a gift from Iowa's soybean growers, and plan a day trip or a family vacation right here in Iowa.

We have also included information about Iowa's Hawk-I insurance program and some tips for parents to help develop your child's reading skills.

We know from recent brain research that 85% of a child's brain is developed in the first six years of life. Reading to small babies and young children helps stimulate their brains and prepares them to learn to read. Just think, today, you may be reading this book to your children, but in a year or two, they'll be reading it to you.

Many people, companies, organizations and departments of state government make it possible for my literacy foundation, Iowa Stories 2000, to give this book to 42,000 children and teachers. I'd like to extend a special thanks to Iowa's Area Education Agencies, who deliver the book to every public and private school in the state. I'd also like to thank Iowa Telecom and Grinnell Verizon employees and their friends and families for helping to distribute the books and assemble the related materials.

I give this book to 42,000 Iowa families to connect us as a larger community of people who share common values. Feeling connected and sharing a common purpose will enable us to raise another generation of young Iowans who may well want to stay here to live, work, play and raise their families.

Sincerely,

Christie Vilsack
First Lady of Iowa

*Please read to a child.
It may be the best part
of your day.*

The Pickle Patch Bathtub

Tricycle Press   Berkeley/Toronto

by Frances Kennedy ~ illustrations by Sheila Aldridge

It was the second Saturday in January when Donna Delle discovered her legs were too long.

In her family's farmhouse kitchen, six miles south of Luray, Missouri, Donna declared, "We need a real bathtub."

"We need to spend our money on more important things," Mama said as she took another teakettle of steaming hot water from the cookstove and poured it into the washtub.

Donna tested the temperature, added a dipper of cold water from the kitchen sink pump, and stepped in. "My legs are too long, and this old tub is too small," she complained.

THE KANSAS CITY STAR.

OL. 45.   NO. 141.   * * *

KANSAS CITY, FEBRUARY 8, 1925—SUNDAY.

In 8 Sections, Including
Magazine and Comic.

PRICE 5 C

ONG TO MOTOR DEBUT   THE WEATHER.   H GAVE

THE DEAD.

C. WODELL, 320 South
ue, engineer on the pas-

NO HOPE OF LIFE

It was the first Sunday in February. The dishes were done, and Papa was taking his after-dinner rest while Mama read him the news from the *Kansas City Star*. Donna gathered her sisters and brother in the front parlor. She opened the Sears, Roebuck catalog and read,

"This tub is made of steel with a heavy metal lining. Is strong and durable. Easy to keep clean. Will last a lifetime. No farmhouse is complete without the luxury of one of our bathtubs. Price: $9.25."

"Let's ask Papa for a real bathtub," said Hazel. "He would want our farm complete."

"I don't think that will work. Mama already said no," sighed Donna.

"And Papa is saving for a new tractor," said Carlyle. "He told me so."

"Nine dollars and twenty-five cents is a lot of money," said Lois.

"And doesn't it cost something for shipping?" asked Alice.

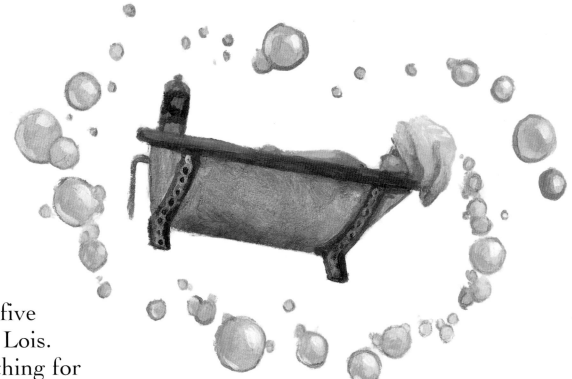

Donna turned the pages of the catalog until she found the order blanks. "A dollar fifty more," she moaned.

No one said a word.

"I was hoping to put the rose soap and talcum powder that Aunt Maud gave me next to the tub," said Donna, "for anyone to use."

No one said a word.

"Helen Watson said her daddy is buying her mama a new tub when he harvests his corn next fall," said Donna, trying again.

"It *would* be nice to have a bathtub before Helen does," said Alice slowly. "But how can we get that much money?"

Donna plopped an empty jelly jar on top of the catalog. "I have a plan. Let's all enter the county fair poetry contest. If we win, and if we all save our Christmas money and birthday money, we can buy a real bathtub."

"I don't write poems, and I don't like baths," said Carlyle. "I fit just fine in our washtub. I'm saving my money to buy a banana when we go to town. Maybe a tarantula will crawl out of the bunch like last time."

Donna ignored her little brother and dropped her Christmas dime in the jar.

Christmas money 5 dimes = 50¢

birthday money 5 dimes = 50¢

Weeding the pasture / 15 cents

Picking Cherries, Strawberries, blackberries 7 cents a pint

Winning the Poetry Contest

two dollars!!!

Chelicerae
Eyes
Tarsus
Carapace
Tibia
Femur
Abdomen
Spinnerets

It was the fourth Friday in March. Donna had come to town to help Papa bring in the eggs and buy coffee and flour for Mama. No one had written a poem, and there was still only one dime in the jelly jar when Donna saw the sign in Hendrick's Produce window. The big, bold letters said:

Wanted

Cucumbers for Pickling
Free Seeds

The Keokuk Cannery
606 Water Street
Keokuk, Iowa

On the way home from town, Donna took a deep breath and said without stopping, "Papa, my legs are getting longer and the washtub is getting smaller and if I grew pickles there would be enough money for a real bathtub and our farm would be complete."

"We'll see," said Papa.

In April, Donna wrote for free seeds, and when they arrived in May, Papa hitched up Topsy and Nellie and plowed last year's hog lot. Then Donna, Alice, Lois, and with the sometime help of Hazel and Carlyle, planted the seeds.

"Remember," said Donna, patting seven fat, white cucumber seeds in the soft, brown hills of soil, "it's
   one for the cutworm,
     one for the crow,
       one for the beetle,
         and four to grow."

In June, Donna's legs were still getting longer, but so were the cucumber vines. The prickly runners with curly pigtail tendrils spread out, coloring the hog lot green.

There wasn't much to do now but wait, and wait, and wait. Then, one day, there it was, a yellow blossom!

In July, the little cucumbers set on, and once there were two whole bushel baskets full, Donna and Papa drove to town. The Keokuk Cannery man dumped the cucumbers on the long sorting table and pushed them through holes of different sizes so they fell into the baskets below.

Donna was disappointed because big cucumbers were not worth nearly as much as the small ones. "It's going to take a lot of cucumbers to buy a bathtub."

August was hot, and working in the sun made Alice feel faint. Hazel and Carlyle were scolded for stepping on the vines.

"I don't like baths and now I don't like cucumbers," said Carlyle. "Neither do I," declared Hazel, and they left to play.

The striped cucumber beetle

The Spotted Cucumber beetle

Donna and Lois had to protect their arms from cucumber prickles and the hot sun. They picked cucumbers in the early morning and yellow beetles long into the afternoon. There were so many cucumbers Papa made two trips to town each week, but the jelly jar was only half full.

In September, Donna was too tired to even count pickle money. Now there was school to attend, wood to bring in, water to pump, homework to do, and always, always, cucumbers to pick.

On October fifteenth, the first killing frost left the vines limp and mushy. Papa took the last bushel of cucumbers to town.

When he returned, Donna counted nine dollars and twenty-five cents into a pile. "This will pay for the bathtub." She pushed it aside and started on a second pile.

Donna put down five quarters. "One dollar and twenty-five cents," added two nickels, "thirty-five," and five more pennies, "thirty-six, thirty-seven, thirty-eight, thirty-nine, and forty."

"We still need ten more cents," said Lois.

"Maybe you made a mistake," said Alice.

Donna pushed all the money into one pile and counted again. "There's not enough money," she said sadly, dropping the coins one at a time back into the jar.

Carlyle reached into the front pocket of his overalls, where he kept his Christmas dime safe. He held it tight in his fist. "There probably aren't any tarantulas in the bananas anyway," he said. "Tommy Johnson got to go to town three times this summer. He told me he didn't see one spider in the whole store."

Carlyle opened his hand slowly and placed the dime on the table.

Just before Halloween, Papa took Donna to the post office to get a money order. Donna carefully counted out nine dollars and twenty-five cents of the pickle patch money for the bathtub and another dollar fifty for shipping. Papa watched as Donna filled out the money order and order form, popped them in an envelope, sealed it, and dropped it in the mail slot.

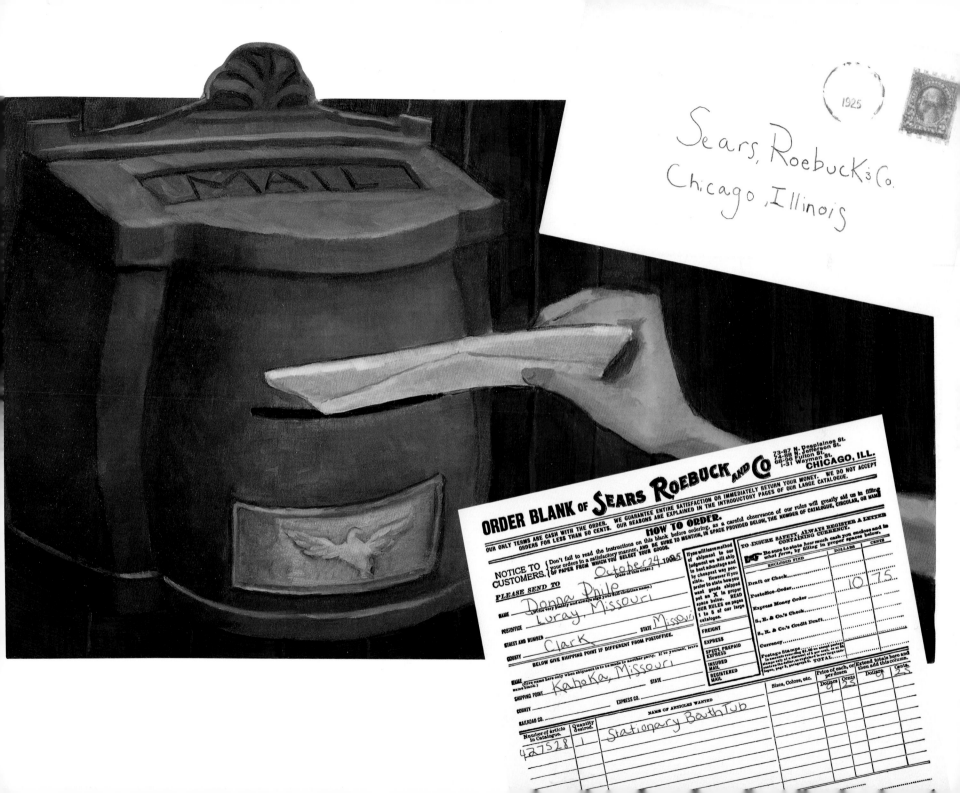

On the third Wednesday in November, the bathtub arrived, but Papa was still busy harvesting the corn. The bathtub sat boarded up in its crate by the back door, waiting.

"After Thanksgiving," promised Papa.

And so it was on the second Saturday night in December at 8:25 p.m. that Mama poured in one last steaming teakettle of water. Donna tested the temperature with her big toe, added a dipper of cold water, stepped into the real bathtub, and found out her legs were not too long after all.

December 12, 1925

Author's Note

Helen Watson and Donna Philp, 1923

My Mother, Donna Delle Philp, was born in Wayland, Missouri, September 20, 1915. When she was four years old, she moved with her father, Frank, her mother, Frances, and her younger sisters, Alice and Lois, to a farm without a bathtub.

The family grew. Hazel and Carlyle were born. On Saturday nights, the whole family took their baths beside the kitchen cookstove in a round galvanized tub that was only ten and a half inches high and twenty-three inches across, and every Monday morning the Philp family laundry was rinsed in the same tub.

Times were hard. The Philp children grew cucumbers for the Keokuk Canning Company. With the money they earned, they purchased a claw-footed metal bathtub.

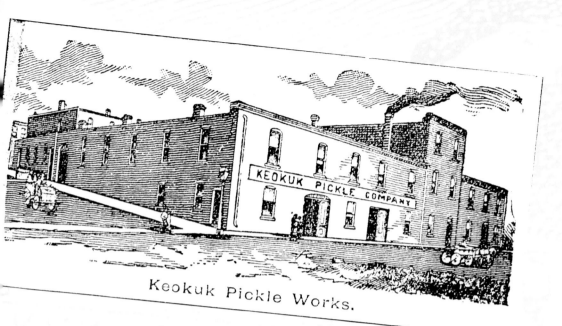

Keokuk Pickle Works.

Bread + Butter Pickles

Slice pickles + onions + soak in salt water 3 hr.

Rinse pickles +
Make 1 cup vinegar, 1 cup water + 1 cup sugar. Let boil with a bag of pickling spice.

Put in pickles let get hot but do not boil

The tub was placed in a storeroom. There was no indoor plumbing, so bath water still had to be heated on the cookstove and carried to the tub. The bath water drained into the backyard. Electricity and many other modern conveniences became a part of life on the farm, but for over forty years, that bathtub and those bathing rituals remained the same.

Donna resided in Sioux City, Iowa, from the early 1940s until her death in 2001. There, she had indoor plumbing and a pink bathtub. Almost all of her ten grandchildren and thirteen great-grandchildren have taken a bath in that pink tub.

Bread and butter pickles were Donna's favorite.

For Mom—FK
To Larry Roberts, the best dad to ever come out of Missouri—SA

TRICYCLE PRESS
a little division of Ten Speed Press
P.O. Box 7123
Berkeley, California 94707
www.tricyclepress.com

Design by Randall Heath / Additional design by Katy Brown
Typeset in Cochin, Victorian, and Courier / The illustrations in this book were rendered in oil/acrylic collage.

Picture Credits
Newspaper: printed with permission from *The Kansas City Star*; Schoolhouse: courtesy of Margaret Walser, Dubuque, Iowa
Order form: courtesy of Sears Brands, LLC; Author's Note/recipe card and Helen and Donna: from the archives of Donna Philp Sisson
Author's Note/Keokuk Pickle Works: courtesy of Lee County, Iowa Historical Society

Library of Congress Cataloging-in-Publication Data
Kennedy, Frances, 1937-
The pickle patch bathtub / by Frances Kennedy ; illustrations by Sheila Aldridge.   p. cm.
Summary: Complaining of legs grown too long for the kitchen washtub, a farm family's children set out to earn enough money for a real bathtub.
ISBN 1-58246-112-0 hc / ISBN 1-58246-174-0 pbk
[1. Moneymaking projects—Fiction. 2. Farm life—Fiction. 3. Cucumbers—Fiction. 4. Bathtubs—Fiction.] I. Aldridge, Sheila, ill. II. Title.
PZ7.K3782 Pi 2004   [E]—dc22   2003017055

Iowa Stories 2000 edition printed in 2006
First Tricycle Press printing, 2004
Printed in China